Florence Page Jaques (1890-1972) was a poet and nature writer. She collaborated with her husband, Francis Lee Jaques, one of America's foremost nature artists, on numerous books for adults. She also wrote stories and nonsense verse for children, including her best-known poem, "There Once Was a Puffin," which was inspired by a letter from her husband describing the puffins he had seen while on a voyage to the Arctic.

Shari Halpern grew up in Needham, Massachusetts, and attended the Rhode Island School of Design. She has illustrated numerous books for children. She lives in New Jersey with her family.

There Once Was a Puffin

By Florence Page Jaques
Illustrated by Shari Halpern

North
South

Oh, there once was a Puffin
Just the shape of a muffin,

And he lived on an island
In the
    bright
        blue
            sea!

He ate little fishes
That were most delicious,

And he had them for supper
And he
  had
    them
      for tea.

But this poor little Puffin,

He couldn't play nothin'

For he hadn't anybody
To
   play
     with
       at all.

So he sat on his island,
And he cried for a while, and
He felt very lonely,
And he
    felt
        very
            small.

Then along came the fishes,
And they said, "If you wishes,
You can have us for playmates,
Instead
    of
        for
            tea!"

So they now play together

In all sorts of weather,

And the Puffin eats pancakes,
Like you
   and
      like
        me.

To Ali, oh Ali, bird expert,
fish expert, and pancake expert,
and special thanks to Joe
—S.H.

Illustrations copyright © 2003 by Shari Halpern
First published in the United States, Great Britain, Canada, Australia, and New
Zealand in 2003 by NorthSouth Books, Inc., an imprint of NordSüd Verlag AG,
CH-8005 Zürich, Switzerland. This edition published in 2015 by NorthSouth Books.
Distributed in the United States by NorthSouth Books, Inc., New York 10016.
Library of Congress Cataloging-in-Publication Data is available.
Printed in China by Leo Paper Products Ltd., Heshan, Guangdong, October 2015.
ISBN: 978-0-7358-4245-8
1 3 5 7 9 · 10 8 6 4 2
www.northsouth.com